I0745728

TIME

microfiction and prose poems

edited by

Cassandra Atherton

SPINELESS WONDERS

www.shortaustralianstories.com.au

Spineless Wonders

PO Box 220

STRAWBERRY HILLS

New South Wales, Australia, 2012

shortaustralianstories.com.au

First published by Spineless Wonders 2018

Cover image and design by Richard Holt

Editorial assistance by Jessica Stewart. Publicity by Katherine Potter. Layout by Bronwyn Mehan.

Typeset in Franklin Gothic Book

Printed and bound by Ingram Spark

ISBN 978-1-925052-35-0

Catalogue-in-print

A823.4

Time, prose poems and microfiction/

Atherton, Cassandra (ed)

TIME

microfiction and prose poems

This project has been assisted by the Australian Government through the Australia Council, its arts funding and advisory body.

Time flies over us, but leaves its shadow behind.

NATHANIEL HAWTHORNE

Contents

Introduction

Humanity has always been obsessed with time – we waste time, lose time, seize time; time flies, it is a thief, it is like the wind or a handful of sand. In postmodern society, we are consumed by ways to save time, multi-task, preserve our youth and prolong our lives. And we are still transfixed by the idea of a time machine that can take us either forward or backward in time. But while others have argued that microliterature is growing in popularity because we are busier than ever before, and microliterature is short and can be read during fractured moments between work and play, they are denying the power of microliterature to engage on a deeper level. The friction of distance is lessened by microliterature's shortness – it fits on one page - and invites immediacy and intimacy, rather than superficiality, in rapidly experienced narratives and metaphor.

Many anthropologists and geographers have argued that since the turn of the century, in particular, globalism and technology have caused our sense of time to be so squeezed that the present is constantly crowding us, both temporally and spatially. This experience of compressed living and the almost oxymoronic immensity that stems from this, can be said to find voice in contemporary microliterature. This is because microliterature is a form which turns on its economy of expression and appeal to time – but also, visually and spatially, in its containment. In this anthology, writers were given a word limit of 200 words or less, which resulted in writing that captured a certain dynamism of space. In this way, microliterature has the effect of onrushing momentum for the reader in a way that mirrors what Harvey identifies as "the marked and debilitating acceleration in the pace of life and of a sense of the future as rushing towards us out of control." Time in microliterature mirrors life or perhaps even entrapment in a postmodern society which is relentlessly compressed and present. However, this compression keeps microliterature energised and intimate and speaks to the fast-paced, future geared sense of living in a post-modern society. While time is condensed in microliterature - both in the act of reading and in the expression of time - it expands outwards, connecting to webs of ideas and meanings beyond the page. In all these ways, time and microliterature are ideal companions.

For this anthology, we suggested to writers that their take on time may be philosophical or flippant, sage or satirical, cross-cultural or curmudgeonly. They might riff on the many everyday time-based aphorisms - just in time, no time to lose, tempus fugit - or take a longer view of time, reflecting on the Anthropocene epoch or time immemorial. The microliterature in this anthology is a rich mix of all these approaches and more, it ranges across many short forms of writing: flash fiction, prose poetry, postcard fiction and nonfiction vignettes. What became apparent in reading the submissions was the need for many writers to express their political sentiments in this form of writing, as if the short form could encourage activism in its intensity and presence. In this way, there are some brilliant pieces on the more political associations with time like climate change, the refugee crisis and terrorism, but also microliterature which turns on identity politics or the politicisation of space. Importantly, there are witty pieces of microliterature on toenail clippings and fries alongside more whimsical ones on Valencia oranges and the sun vanishing in the evening. They have been arranged in this anthology as a kind of interweaving of dark and light threads to form a tapestry of responses to time.

Congratulations to those shortlisted for the Newcastle Writers Festival/joanne burns Microlit award and to all of the writers who entered the competition. It was an almost impossible process shortlisting entries as there were so many accomplished and compelling pieces: all of them responded to the theme with enthusiasm and creativity. The two winning pieces are Traces by Tess Pearson (National category) and Luke Evans (Hunter category). These tightly crafted pieces of microliterature are memorable for their quirky originality in their exploration of the theme, and for their brilliant control in this short form.

Thank you to Rosemarie Milsom, director of the Newcastle Writers Festival for her incredible support and for extending this award to the Newcastle Writers Festival. It is a wonderful festival environment in which to discuss such a diverse and popular form of writing.

Thank you to the commissioned writers: Dael Allison, Julie Chevalier, Eileen Chong, Shady Cosgrove, Tim Heffernan, Richard Holt, Andy Jackson, Lee Kofman, Catherine Noske and Paul Munden for their stunning writing which traverses a range of forms and approaches to microliterature and time. A special thank you to many of writers here who were not experienced in this form but were willing to experiment with something new.

Thank you to Jessica Stewart for her editorial assistance and to Katherine Potter for her assistance with publicity. And huge thanks to Richard Holt for his brilliant noir cover design of time-lapse as well as his memorable piece of writing in this anthology. Thank you to joanne burns, who lends her name to this award and is a pioneer in Australia for microliterature. Finally, thank you to Spineless Wonders' publisher, Bronwyn Mehan. The short form is a flourishing but often overlooked form in Australia and Spineless Wonders has provided me, as series editor of these anthologies, with an important platform for championing the form and providing writers with incredible opportunities to be published in new and exciting ways.

Cassandra Atherton, 2018

Tess Pearson

TRACES

I once found one of your toenail clippings, years later, down the side of the couch. It was definitely yours. There was no mistaking it. The moment collapsed in on itself, a union of repulsion and yearning. A second later: pure annoyance. *Couldn't you have cut your toenails outside?* Like an afterimage, I kept seeing the shape of your big toe. In the end I buried it in the garden, the way I'd bury dead pet mice and goldfish when I was a child. Only, without any flowers on top.

Catherine Noske

OLIVER

In the kitchen, the kitten arches his back and leans against your legs, hangs between them like a child might. I leave you together to enjoy your breakfast, but he follows, breaks into the bathroom to watch me shower, head to one side, like I watched you.

He is an indoors cat. He stretches with me on the couch, body to my belly, one eye on the window as you pot basil outside. The world is blue and gold. You eat an apple like a horse might, fumbling pieces in full-mouth enjoyment, holding it well clear, your free hand dirt-tipped and damp with blood-and-bone. I imagine a child squatting beside you, mouth open in witness to your dexterity. The kitten falls asleep.

At the doctor's office, the same sunshine is sterilised and hung on the wall with her degrees. I leave with one hand to the emptiness, knowing what I knew already, but somehow more. You drive in silence. At home, the kitten will be waiting, tin-ribbed and needy for us.

Eileen Chong

GREEN GRIEF

I heard about your wedding in a Catholic church so much food and wine live jazz band how you'd lost all that weight everyone so happy. Revenge fantasies: you fell off a cliff got run over by a truck you were buried up to your neck drizzled with honey and left for the ants your plane went down over the Pacific you had a heart attack you were shot in the eye. You see, poets have this thing for truth. The memory of crying so hard I threw up but in the shower so you wouldn't hear though there was no door on the bathroom. My therapist says I had a choice I probably was the problem I couldn't be the woman who would sit down and shut up or stand in a cupboard all day waiting until you got home and unlocked it. In my dream you were in my house and my friend who is also a poet said I have to tell you to vacate the premises because you would never ever acknowledge what you did to me. Larkin said *Last year is dead* and to *Begin afresh, afresh, afresh.* Repetition here is key.

Mark O'Flynn

TRACES OF NUTS

Allergic to the twentieth century and particularly peanut butter the killer swelled up, sneezed, grew pestilential scabs. Hospitalised on more than one occasion after contact with flouride, pesticides, hairspray, bread, or any product containing traces of nuts they performed a tracheotomy to grant him breath. Saved for greater things, he said. On Death Row his allergies eased, the diet agreeable, the air innocuous. The hangman came to weigh him, placed latex hands about his neck. For the last meal, when the time came, allergic to life, he ordered peanut butter.

Julie Chevalier

AMERICAN PHOTOGRAPHER FAILS TO SNAP AUSTRALIAN NIGHT PARROT

'I carry little equipment. Taking three giant steps forward is quicker and less intrusive than screwing on a telephoto lens,' Diane Arbus told fellow wildlife photographers. She showed little interest in rows of Australian night parrots preserved in drawers at the Australian Museum, 'like on a contact sheet.'

'I've heard that paparazzi are more likely to kill a night parrot with a Land Rover than to shoot one in spinifex. I'm relieved you don't eat parrots. I wasn't sure.'

'Famous endangered birds are entitled to their privacy and shouldn't have to primp and pose for the camera. Retouching beaks with lipstick is abhorrent.'

Ideal subjects, according to the photographer, are shipwrecked, alcoholic, addicted, incarcerated or deformed birds. She likes to photograph one-legged cross-dressing crows wearing eye patches and garters, obese cockatoos with tattoos, and bald eagles wearing asymmetrical flamingo-feather wigs.

'I bet there are fascinating species in bedrooms from Come By Chance to Wagga Wagga,' said Arbus, who will vote Celibate in the coming election.

Kim Waters

OVER TIME

Every weekend, he rode miles up and down the Great Ocean Road, a flask of water clipped to the bike frame, his helmet bobbing in regular breaths. Now he sits in a brown leather chair working the lever at his side, searching for the right elevation, the perfect tipping point for a glass of beer on the TV's horizon.

Sometimes it's hard to join the dots between the years. The points seem out of alignment, and although you look for logic in the harlequin patterns, there's nothing there but a dark tunnel with only the palest stream of light hissing in the distance.

Andy Jackson

THAT PHOTOGRAPH

I open the envelope, arrange all the pages of my adolescent medical file across the desk, the bed, the floor. If I could see each and every recorded note and image at once – the mapping of heart function, blood pressure, bowel movements, how I described my pain back then – I might find some way to reconcile that time with this. The nurses' handwriting is cryptic, ambiguous. *Light sleeper. Somewhat stooped. Co-operative. Responds to encouragement.* And there I am, twelve, barely flinching in the flash of the camera. Its clinical lens. This poorly photocopied image, all exposure and shadow. A singular person, blurred, nakedly soft. He stands there, unmoving, as I circle him, looking back in time. I catch a foot on the curve of his rib and fall. Chest-deep in this, struggling, I'm sinking, as if awake under anaesthetic, powerless. I can only watch, as a thin and startled boy wanders around the house. Trapped, I look out from within that photo.

Quinn Eades

WHAT GROWS

While hair grows on my belly and chin and legs and the underside of my forearms and toes, it recedes on my head. I have two sharp triangles pointing backwards from my forehead. A burnished orange koi swims down my right forearm. Its head has always been velvety smooth, but now it is hairy too. This is how I measure time and transition: hair appearing and disappearing. Finding newly smooth places. Counting months while belly hair moves up to meet my chest scars. Waiting to see what will fall and what will stay.

Dominique Hecq

FOUR THOUSAND WINKS

I was born one night in spring. My mother, panting abortively at each gasp, later convinced me of my angelhood. At first I failed to cry, my scarlet complexion announcing to the world that I was withholding my breath. Then I wailed and wailed. Closed my mouth on a dummy. I jiggled my arms and shoulders, hips and legs. Wriggled my toes. All according to plan. A closet explorer, I had already tasted blood and water, sugar and salt. I had heard and listened to Barbara's throat vibrations, tummy gurgles and the mysterious *thud thud* that shook us once a week. I had felt for an exit, and found it. My hands tracked down my toes. Pulled at my hair. I crawled. Stood. Walked. Ran. I tried to fly. Fell in the spacetime of childhood.

Venita Munir

TIME TO LEAVE

He's always there. Perhaps I'm being paranoid. There's no menace and we like similar music. We eke out the work hours in banter.

He starts to loiter around Emergency, though rostered to the wards. Doesn't approach me, but looms present without any tasks. It seems unusual, but orderlies can work hospital-wide. He's distinct; the blond ponytail of a surfer, but pallid and willowy like he lives on *2-Minute Noodles* in a vegan share house.

Crossing the gritty carpark at night always unnerves me. After my late shift I find him tinkering under his old beetle. His familiarity reassures me, until I realise he finished hours ago. He's sheepish. Invites me to see a band with him.

I smirk, shrug and say, 'I have a boyfriend.'

I drive out the boomgate, his beetle follows, its beady eyes in my mirror all the way home.

Imagining he's at my window, I don't sleep.

Next morning I confront him. He flaps in denial.

I receive odd phone-calls, a card reading, 'In Good Time', a CD sporting phallic mushrooms on the cover.

I must move, house and job. Change numbers.

Later, he appears.

In my new workplace.

Beams.

'Found you.'

Luke Evans

YOU CAN'T GO HOME AGAIN

My feet hit the ground and I stepped away from the bus. I took a deep breath and sighed out the air and all that it meant. There was nobody waiting for me. I wasn't surprised; I hadn't told anyone I was returning and I'd been away for nine years.

I grew up in this old industrial town and I loved it instinctively as the place where I had started. That was a long time ago. Now, as I looked at it, I couldn't remember why I had loved it.

It was empty and somehow lacking. The industries on which the city was founded had abandoned her for greener pastures. Shops stood empty, buildings run down. Graffiti covered their walls and marked them as damaged. And here I stood, older, jaded and lost, but for reasons that I didn't really understand; I had come home.

We were both somehow hollow; lost lovers pushed back together. I looked at the empty storefronts and I knew she was empty, too. I turned back to the bus, with the thought of riding it until the end of the line.

The bus was gone.

Luke Fussell

THE ROO-SHOOTER

My father was a roo-shooter and my boys will probably do the same thing. Sitting alone in this cabin, I wonder, would I do this if I had the choice again? My father sat in this chair pushing his dinner around the plate, listening to the moaning generator, but I don't know if he ever had second thoughts because he never said a word. It was just a job and he did it. It probably sounds weird to a city bloke, but out here in the dark, I know every turn in the track like I'm doing a milk-run in the fuckin' suburbs.

A few months back a film crew came out here and followed me 'round for a few days. They wanted to see what it was like for someone like me. They were kids from the university, kids who wanted to be directors or something. *Authenticity*, they kept saying. They came to find *authenticity*. They also called me a dying breed, and they're probably right. These roos pop-up quicker than I can shoot 'em. And one day I'll be dead, but the roos will be out here dodging the next shooter.

Emma Homes

MUNURRU

In the morning they saw the trees and the river with the blue dome of sky overhead, and decided not to travel on.

They swam. The children jumped from rocks. Splashed and scolded each other. The man strummed a guitar. The woman mended her broken sandal. Freshwater crocodiles basked nearby.

When the sun was high they drove out of the campground, along the dusty corrugated road, and parked next to a small bus. They wandered between trees and long grass to a congregation of boulders.

There were spirits painted, and bones.

Two brolgas. An echidna. Wandjina. A child's hand.

They took photographs, posing in front of the paintings. Told the children to move if they stood too close.

The family loitered near the tour group.

... 'human and god-like qualities' ... 'bring the wet season's rain' ... 'evolved over thousands of years'

There was a low cave, with tree roots like pillars. The woman sat beneath the press of rock and waited for the others to move away.

She traced a finger in the dust. Listened.

In the morning they drove away.

Deborah Van Heekeren

TIME OF DEATH

We travelled through the cold valley to mark her death. Entered from the northern day to where a soul had passed away. Into a wintery land. Damp, and English green, at the solstice of the antipodes. We passed a ghostly chorus line that twirled and turned across the way. Along the dark horizon, white birds with rhythmic wings. Beating out of time. Forever out of time. We left behind the sleeping stone, amongst fruit trees standing dormant. Without leaves. In a pattern of torment. Without movement. Stilled, chilled at her time of death.

Lee Kofman

PERMANENCE

Television again sings an opera of gunfire. People will always shoot people, we just never believe it. Your eyes are empty of me. I forget what it feels like a foreign skin on my skin. I know tomorrow will be empty of you, but my television is full of affordable romance. I will be that woman you see every day on your crowded way home – looming large above our flickering, electronic city; her diamonds are on sale and on her ring finger. I like her smile, photoshopped and longlasting. Permanence is just something we never believe in.

Shady Cosgrove

SELF-MEDICATION

At the supermarket, you haven't made it past the trolleys and you're yelling at your partner. Half the problem, at least, must be yours, so you sign up to a yoga website and start getting up at 6am. Your downward dog is a creaky old thing, blind and stiff. But you stick with it. Doesn't make sense – stretching and silence, that's all – but you now you can appreciate the distant hum of traffic and the smell of cut grass.

But then they're talking about redundancies at work and you're up at five-thirty, then five am. Your purple mat on the floorboards, your reflection in the dark windows. This helps, but your father gets sick and now it's four am. The tax bill is running late: three. Sleep is overrated, you tell yourself, legs lifting for a headstand. When you've mastered wheel pose, your sessions are starting before midnight. And it's only a matter of time before you're hitting the mat when everyone else hits bed.

Kathleen Bleakley

LOADED FRIES

would you like fries with that? no, thanks. i'm buying tissues. boxes full. i've been weeping since john wayne galloped back into our living rooms. *not gonna let any more yellows, browns or blacks into our frontiers*, he said. that morning people woke from long slumber. they'd od-ed on masses of super processed creamy crispy donuts. when they woke john wayne was on tv. *would you like fries with that?* i'm buying tissues. boxes full. i've been weeping since the crowning of the new president. people bought loads of coke & toasted him. waved flags. hung them on their front fences & cars. *would you like fries with that?* i've been weeping since i started picking up coke cans from green spaces & creeks. on the beach & in the ocean. they've started building another mega store. there used to be a nursery there. we'd walk down, come back with armfuls of plants. next time I'm asked *would you like fries with that?* i'll say *no thanks, i'll have seeds.*

Andrew Roff

THE LOST HOUR

Heaven is too crowded for Agnes' taste. For the solitude, she frequents the lost hour: that missing beat at the start of summer when modern clocks leap forward, and old ones nag for a winding.

The time foregone falls between two and three a.m., and most of the living would have given the minutes over to sleep. Agnes, a librarian pre- and post-mortem, catalogues what else has been surrendered: arguments (Dewey: 168.1), late-night snacks (641.3), unaired infomercials (659.1). Children scheduled for conception during that hour will never exist; drunken declarations of love will remain unuttered. Agnes weeps as she works, flipping through index cards for a destroyed collection.

An hour is added at the end of summer, to balance the ledger. But that is a different hour, an artifice, full of unrelated happenings. For those who need what was omitted, it is no recompense. They are ignorant, but Agnes takes note: the DJ not reviewed, never discovered; the hotel cook, fatigued, who scorches her hand against the grill; the condemned man marking off the days.

The stretch spent living is already too short. Now that she has time in abundance, Agnes knows the folly of daylight saving.

Johanna Ellersdorfer

TEXTING THROUGH TIME ZONES

'Good morning', I type, curling into bed and pulling the blankets around me, the day racing through my mind and out of my fingertips in a quick series of harried text messages buzzing gently along with your morning alarm. A compressed version of my day ending and yours starting, summarised in a mutually punctuated stream of consciousness, framed by tiny blue and white bubbles on a phone screen approximating, but always falling short of where I've actually been and what you've actually done.

Marjorie Lewis-Jones

SALAMANCA SPYHOLE

Salamanca spyhole: glazed nipple. Smear of calligrapher's ink.
Glair from the last trick trashed. Who's next?
Whisky eyes hitched in a moth-eaten hallway. Crushed lips. Sagged bed. Remember when the girl jumped? Faces go in waves. Rippling wormholes. The glass dredged. Shagged bodies beached.
She needs pummelling—after it. (Differently.) Knuckle to spine. Pumice to sour skin. Dawn's a spit away. Her boy: a bus ride. Curls tacky. Teat hollow: stiff at his cheek.
Slipping from the sheets to cross the room from the slumbering men the night sunders. Splits her like a stick. Stealth smooths her into wallets—running a thumb over the wads, and lifting what's hers, what's owed, what's left.
It's less than she needs.
Go now, she whispers to her feet, as the lobby spills her into the bleak morning. *Faster*, she begs the bus—as if it will help—though *it must*. He'll be screaming now. Wet. If the neighbour twigs he's alone, she'll call the cops. And, if they get there before her, that will be that.

Brianna Bullen

NOSTALGIC LEISURE INDUSTRY

You sign up for the *Nostalgic Leisure Experience* because the memory industry seems more real than the present. Memory is, presently, the only proven form of time-travel, outside of imagination and kissing. You're surprised to find they have your files, and have organised your life in terms of objects. You don't ask how they got them, but happily collect the bulging sack they give you. Lost time hoarded in a handbag, in Proust's madeleines and the punk CDs you used to listen to in your teens. The image of her chap-stick smile. A postcard dated from six years ago, *wishing you were here*. Your red gumboots you could never quite chuck out. Old sketches of your Jack Russells, superimposed with their fates: snake bite, car wheel, old age. You dreamt of working with kakapos, prehistoric birds out of time. That version of you smeared out of reality by quantum choice, divergent branch snipped. Old letters to lovers, archaic but material; Facebook posts, time-stamped. They have nothing for recent years, only a black cloud cut-out and some files from work, all repeating meaningless personally meaningless numbers. Cheeky. You sign up for the more expensive deluxe option.

Arna Radovich

HERE WE ARE

I sat on the cold concrete bench trying to avoid the pigeon droppings and remnants of blackened gum, and sipped my flat white slowly. It made me feel sick but I drank it anyway, just to insist that everything was normal. Milky and weak, it was more like the cappuccinos they made in the early days, before baristas and soy lattes and macchiatos or those coffee beans that are pooped by civets. I read an online article about it—kopi luwak they call it—it was right next to a story about chemical bombing in Syria. I had a dream that night, a nightmare really, about caged civets like battery hens being force-fed coffee cherries. Rows and rows of civets, their weasily muzzles pressed against the bars, long brush tails curled around their contorted bodies, staring at the world with their tortured no-hoper eyes—their lives a sepia of quiet desperation, a sign—like a canary in a coal mine—of the times we live in.

Catherine Deery

FISH CASSEROLE

She holds her teacup with two hands and sips. Jim lifts the loose skin on his forearm between finger and thumb, releases, lifts again. The fish casserole sits on the table between them, sweating under the plastic wrap. He's saying something about the sale going through Monday. 'Better to be with family.' He twists his little finger in his ear, pulls it out and examines it.

She looks away, then places the cup back down in the saucer. The children under the table have gone quiet. She stands up, puts her handbag on her shoulder.

As she drives away, the sun is low and red in the sky and she breathes heavily through her mouth. Her armpits are wet. At the end of the driveway she does an abrupt U-turn. She drives back, parks under the peppercorn tree, runs to the house, then stops.

Jim is on the veranda, scraping her casserole into the dog bowl. The kelpie is gulping the casserole down greedily. They both look up at her. The dog puts its head down and cleans up the bowl. Jim shrugs.

'Here,' he says, handing her the empty dish. 'Thanks anyway.'

Nimity James

ANNIVERSARY

If you must begin again, take all the things that make up your life. Grab as many of them as you can, be sure to look carefully. A birthday poem, nighttime trysts, red-colossus days, promises of a flowering life and days of silver hues. How you slept and the dreams you had. What your friends thought of you, what you thought of you. How many lies you told. Or didn't. The songs you sang, the dances you danced and who you danced with. You did dance, didn't you? Your pluck, your cowardice, your just plain janeness. Keep going. Take all these things and more. Now – burn them. With the burnt pieces that are left to you reassemble in any way you see fit. What can you make? Whatever it is, it resembles you. It's what you were and what you would become. Now, suck in a lung full of air and blow. See the fragments scatter? Do not collect them. They are no good to you now. They can't save you. You are here. And from here you must begin.

Yvonne Fein

TIME LIES

There was a time when Time was brutally Australian — when we landed on this wide brown land and declared it began only then. Nothing of note: people, culture, song, had occurred before then.

There was a time when Time was peculiarly Australian — elevated almost to mythical status when that towering man of dreams told the nation, 'It's Time!' And yes, it was, but like Camelot, it endured only for one brief shining moment.

Einstein eventually convinced his peers that the dividing line between past, present and future was an illusion. But tell that to lost civilisations around the world whose past was obliterated by the present which ensured the darkness or disappearance of their future.

He was a genius, Einstein, but he did not understand that the beliefs of the Other, sacred, ubiquitous, savage, would impact on his people violently through time. Even though he witnessed the worst of it, he insisted on timelessness.

Those fantasists — Verne, Asimov, Bradbury — all fly us through time. And we follow in their wake, ineluctably drawn to that perilous, that most dishonest of masters.

Julie U'Ren

DETAINED

You could see the sky there; a patch between corrugated iron rooves and cyclone fencing laced with razor wire. Clouds thick, like churned cream hung low in the wet season afternoon. The green frogs chorused loudly as if there might be something nearby- like freedom. I followed staff through gates that clicked open then just as firmly, closed. I waited on a moulded plastic chair in the visiting room pumped with cold air. He'd walk in, eyes twinkling, smiling *hello*. With my pen, he circled the drawing of his family, touching the lines, saying each name, as if that would make them present for a moment. Each time his voice would soften, the light in his eyes dulled. He'd stretch his hands helplessly before me on the table. As I was leaving I noticed the clouds move and separate, yet it was the patch between iron rooves and cyclone fencing that I'd remember.

Dael Allison

RITUAL

Child-gnarly, she sits on the soft-woven pandanus mat, deep in the shadow of the breadfruit tree. She is as still as a Ray Crook painting, fingertips soft from folding petals. Her skin glows the way light can be sucked into dark places. Her head is garlanded for first menstruation, crowned with yellow frangipanis and that white one, *mainaina*, with its scent of forgetting. Behind her the lagoon sheets blue to the horizon's beyond. Tomorrow will be like this day, and the next. She will not look over her shoulder for what she knew before, now that the red flowers have come.

Dorothy Simmons

IN THE AIR

Over 50,000 people are in the air right now. But she's not one of them. On the wall of the departure lounge, the pretty poster child stares endlessly out of the plane window. How much longer?

She glances around: why doesn't the overloaded sky fall in, squash all these chicken lickens? What does right now mean anyway? When it's already right past, no sooner said than gone? How did they count the 50,000? When? How can they know for sure? They could redefine cloud streaming, some kind of cumulo-nimbus conveyer belt... which her father, hands clasped in prayer, bound for glory, would simply rocket straight through. Her dear departed Dad: like that Irish comedian he used to quote, may your God go with you.

Boarding now, they said: five minutes later, please return to your seats. Why? What have they found? Some ticking time bomb? Should she be grateful instead of irate? Isn't it better to be late than... the late?

The gold braided steward is talking to his mobile again. Do we have lift off? Can we join the 50,000?

Boarding passes, please. Finally. Why? No answer. Nobody knows. Nobody ever did.

Christine Burrows

ALUMINIUM SKY

Left hand shielding eyes, he looks up. White sun. Sky no longer blue, but silver above criss-crossing clouds. He remembers a yellow sun he could look directly at in winter when he was a kid. Yellow, in a sapphire blue sky. Now its bleached glare blinds him. Weather programming, he tells her. Aluminium particles twinkle coy like daytime stars. Float invisible, unnoticed, to ground. His throat hurts again today. Mild nausea comes and goes. Everyone in the town feels it. The niggling. Then they forget. Then the niggling. Home-grown veggies don't taste right. Last year's mystery blight is worse this year. Things don't grow properly, though the moon's corona sparkles like a carnival. It's so pretty. Isn't it beautiful? Click. Click. #paradiseishere #rainbowskies. Post. Ten likes, two hearts in one minute. Scroll. Scroll. While an off-course military jet leaves a wire-thin trail, a hair-line fracture from south east to north west, then disappears. Jet? What jet? As if in ultra slow-mo, a straight string of white vapour materialises, gradually spreads away from the horizontal axis. Then, as if detonated, billows out. The clear silver sky becomes a heavy grey cauldron, its curdling mass bubbling under a white sun.

Jennifer Kornberger

NO CLOCK IN THE RENTAL CABIN AT MOORE RIVER

no watch on his wrist or phone in his back pocket. no dope or beer to send him out or under. just the box of food that Lucy had thrust at his chest before he left Perth, hissing, *use the time to do something about yourself*. his only plan to sit next to the winter-fat river and watch it absorb the sky. sit under the tattered scrolls of paperbark and allow seconds to be siphoned from him, minutes to be netted until his blood runs clear of their thrashing, hours rolled off like limestone boulders. he'll become a planet in retrograde, undoing himself to the point where life might teeter forward again. a man who will become more exact without measurement. as he sits the sun eyes him with new interest, scrawls messages in wavering script into the shallows of the tannin-dark river. the river responds by breaking its sand bar at the mouth. he sits facing the fierce tug of rust coloured water as it empties all standard time into the sea.

Sharon Willdin

REVERIE

We went to the site of the trees and shrubs, just before the sand and water's edge, the ropes where they had been captured and held were still visible, frayed and severed, for a moment it looked like the top part of their arms had been cut off. They showed us, without the need for words, that it happened at the bottom of the hill. Two got away and one didn't.

An apparition manifested, wearing the clothes she had been in when she died. Her clothes were not soiled or stained. She looked crisp and fresh and she wore a white linen frock with a gold leaf print. It was modest, with an open neckline, sleeveless, gathered at the waist, and the length fell between her knees and her calves. She had long mousy brown hair, a polished plain face and high cheekbones. She showed us a vision of her on top of the ridge, sitting on a bicycle, with her dress pulled up on the left-hand side.

I assume she was taken from the site where they had all been tied up, put in the hessian bag and ferried to the island, across the dark waters, in a small row boat, and it must have been there that she was killed.

Emma Ashmere

THE HISTORIC PRESENT

Today's first box delivered to the reading room. Inside, a slip of blue paper. Standard issue, Melbourne Gaol. The believer to the murderess: *Salvation will smile upon your face.*

Second: *Irish girl extinguishes herself in the Yarra. Recalcitrant. Immigrant Depot. Runaway.* Swimming home.

Third: 1867. A farming woman's diary, blue sloping hand. Who is she writing to? Her husband has been gone three months. Perhaps to the child kicking beneath her unlaundered skirts.

Fourth: *Madam de Clef, palmist, formerly of. Wanted. Also under the name Miss Dorcas Bunt.*

Fifth: The Clifton Hill milliner's assistant, 1908. Monday to Saturday: *Worked*. Wednesdays, half day: *Had a yarn. Had a bath*. Sundays, *walking out*. In a stolen hat?

Sixth: *Do not leave your dead on the hospital steps. It has come to the attention of. Without visible means of support. Cholera. Three females mistaken for heaps of rags.*

I blink on the State Library steps - hoping - fearing – I'll find men in top hats and women in crinolines tiptoeing through the horses' dust. By the time I've reached the pedestrian lights on the corner of Swanston and Lonsdale, I've already forgotten them. Why then, three heaps of rags huddled at my feet?

Debra Le Nepveu

THE END OF DAYS

We agreed to meet at 1.30 pm under Gaunt's ornate clock in the Royal Arcade. I waited beneath the giant, mythical carvings of Gog and Magog and recalled his hurried morning departure. No time to kiss goodbye.

The clock's sentinels ogled me. I recalled legendary tales that they were evil predictors of imminent disaster.

Suddenly, a cacophony invaded the Arcade. Car tyres screeched. Screams mingled with wailing sirens. People, bloodied, crippled, stumbled into the Arcade from the Bourke Street mall.

Transfixed, I heard Gog and Magog's arms strike the hour, proclaiming he was late.

Richard Holt

MATHS

'Twenty-five years.' Judge Lanning eyed herself in the role of the accused. She peered, over her spectacles, at her own working-too-hard reflection. Her glasses were the black-rimmed kind her father had favoured.

Twenty-five. How old would she be? Almost seventy by the time Loxton could even front the board. Seventy when he was released.

If he was released.

If he lasted that long. Prisoners like him.

Seventy—that couldn't be right. She re-did the maths. Gemma would be thirty-three. Tiny Leah would be twenty-five—that maths, at least, was easy.

She said it out loud this time. 'Life in prison. Parole to be set...' Tailing off into another thought. Loxton would never convince them he was right to be let out. Would he? What he'd done. What he was capable of.

'You're talking to yourself,' said Gemma from the hallway. 'First sign of madness.'

The Judge turned, but not so fast as to betray anything more than a little surprise. Her courtroom face. Perhaps the kid was right. She usually was—she was that sort of kid. Her mother's daughter.

Twenty-five years was a bloody long stretch.

She wondered if it was enough.

Maree Gallop

HOME SEWN

The collar's stiff on Joel's new school shirt. Two buttons have fallen off within first term of Year 11. My amateurish attempts to sew them back on look desperate. Black cotton against a blue shirt. In earlier school years his shirts were cheap, wash and wear, surprisingly sturdy. I do admit to soaking a shirt or two overnight though. Rough play down bottom field. No permanent stains. Now this expensive shirt from the Uniform Shop needs ironing every morning. Clouds of steam hover over the emblem of the blue sailing boat obscuring the yellow guiding star.

Joel drags himself from his bedroom, dressed in this uniform with its threads of black against blue, so obvious. But Joel's never mentioned them. I reach up and pat the emblem over his chest, hoping to create a breeze to fill the sails. His voice crashes, shipwrecked.

'Shirt's too tight.'

When I was a girl, my mum made my uniform. She designed a pattern from my shape then cut pieces of material, pinned and sewed them. She hand-stitched the emblem. Every year she let out the seams and adjusted the hem. My uniform was made to measure.

I pray I've inherited her skill.

Tim Heffernan

ON THE LADDER

the first writing ended in madness, but for twenty years the words stayed in your head trying to find shapes that would speak. this time you return to drafts of delusion, but the draughts of delusion return you to this time. on the ladder you think of what to write, the second coming. at that precise moment the words, the music and the man meld. meaning meets you and you understand the pulse of the place, the beating of hearts, the chorus of uncertainty, the construction from nothing, the coming back to fix the temple, the houses of sticks, the clutching of straws, the building with beaks. sometimes when the writing is good and the music is too it is like you are wired. as you listen, the melody, the lyric, prompts you, supports you, sings your sentence and the breeze pushes you, gives you direction, tells you which way to go, which path to follow. the breeze breathes.

Amanda Berry

IN THE SCHEME OF THINGS

My elongated shadow lies over tussocked sand. Weathered boulders behind me glow red, rocks so full of iron and air that they clang like cathedral bells. The desert is silent, but for the wind that makes imperceptible changes, grains at a time. Distant mountains encompass the veld, banded granite worn into tables for giants. Volcanoes have written their stories here too, long ago, but only a few know how to read them. The sun vanishes with haste. The air glows mauve and rose and turquoise. The ancient mountains are pink, just for a moment. Tomorrow will be the same as it has been forever. Heating and cooling, all crumbling to sand. Tomorrow I won't be here, I leave in the morning. Soon it is so dark that I make no shape. In time, I will exist only in the minds of others and then not at all. A billion stars dazzle and drip from the blackness, so close, so bright. For now I am a part of all this and I am nothing, nothing.

Raelee Lancaster

WHA'D I TELL YA?

They was sittin' round the table with dyed, dried grasses tryin' to make a basket. I climbed up next to Auntie. My feets didn't even touch the ground. I swung 'em back and forth til Auntie tapped my knee and gave me that look. 'Wha'd I tell ya?' Someone handed me some grasses. I never membered how to start and, when I told 'em that, Auntie gave me a good hit up the back of the head and a look again. 'Wha'd I tell ya?' I took my grasses and stared at 'em for a while. I looked up at Auntie and back down at the grasses. The girl next to me swapped her started one for my loose pile and showed me what to do. I pulled the grasses through each loop I made til I felt loopy just the same. I listened to the old ones yarn. About their kids and their kids' kids and the bag lady at Coles. One of 'em called her gwani and another said they wasn't allowed to say that no more. When I finished, I gave my wonky basket to Auntie. She gave me a kiss and said, 'Wha'd I tell ya?'

Shari Kocher

MEDITATION ON TIME AFTER THE DEATH OF MY FATHER

I took the lift. It went up. I'd forgotten which floor I was meant to be on, even though I'd just asked Linda, *One or four?* So first I went up. Nobody there. Then I went down. Stood in the hallway, pondering. What does Number One? What is its character? Then I went inside the lift again. Back to where I thought I was going. Sat in a chair. Owls on my shirt. Too-whit-to-woo. In the dark of morning. Then Lou arrived, with tigers. Round and round the banyan tree. Like butter. Shoes, feet, floor, a certain number of bags. Also under my eyes. A thousand bowls of butter turned to ghee. That's it! With Suzanne and Linda and Lou and me.

Paul Munden

WINTER, 1963

Poole Park lake is so deeply frozen that everyone is venturing onto the ice without a second thought, their workaday shoes and boots pressing a film of water into service, scooting them around an inland sea, in a scene from Breughel, with me holding my mother's hand. The miniature railway—if it hadn't seized—would offer a perfect, circling view of the imbroglio. Instead, there's a few sunlit seconds of ciné film taken by my father from his standpoint on the edge, and some black and white snaps from the longer freeze. In one, I stand outside the kitchen door on a path cleared of snow, ready for my first day at school, in cap and raincoat, holding a drawstring bag (containing what? plimsolls?) and thinking this would be the model for years to come.

Banjo Weatherald

VALENCIA

Today I picked an orange from my backyard tree. The orange was sour. Picked too soon I suppose. Last time you were here the oranges were little green balls like those that hang on Christmas Trees or from the ears of your friend who wore that black dinner dress. That was summer, and there is a photograph of us squinting and eating watermelon. Now it is autumn and the fruit hang like yellow festoon globes. It is cold outside and I wear a plum scarf that you gave me for my birthday when the orange tree was just in blossom. I don't hear from you anymore and in a few weeks the oranges will be sweet. I suppose I will have to eat them all myself.

Biographies

SHARON WILLDIN is an award-winning writer who was raised in regional NSW and currently lives in Sydney. Sharon has studied screenwriting at AFTRS and creative writing at UNSW and the University of Sydney.

BANJO WEATHERALD is writer based in Adelaide. When he is not writing he is singing songs and gardening and sometimes he can be found sleeping on one of the branches of his favourite walnut tree.

KIM WATERS lives in Melbourne where she works part-time and studies music and visual art. Her poems have been published in a number of Australian journals including *Verge*, *Antithesis*, *Offset 16*, *Communion 5* and *Tincture*.

DEBORAH VAN HEEKEREN was born in Sydney and moved to Maitland from the Central Coast in 2013. Recently retired from her academic career in anthropology, she is concentrating on her creative art practice.

JULIE U'REN returned to the Northern Territory after living for many years in Central Victoria. She is curious about how place and people can change us and explores this in her writing. She has been a finalist in the 2016 & 2107 NT Literary Awards. Julie lives in Darwin.

DOROTHY SIMMONS is an Irish-Australian writer and teacher, whose published work includes four YA novels, the historical fiction, *Living like a Kelly (*Australian Scholarly Publishing, 2015) a number of short stories and the microfiction 'On the Hour' (*Out of Place*, Spineless Wonders. 2015).

ANDREW ROFF's first manuscript was shortlisted for the Wakefield Press Unpublished Manuscript Award at the 2016 Adelaide Festival Awards for Literature. His short fiction has appeared in *Antithesis Journal* and *Antipodean SF*. He tweets @roffwrites.

ARNA RADOVICH writes short fiction, children's stories and microlit. Her work has appeared in *FourW-25*: *New Writing*, *ZineWest*, *Islet*, *Verandah*, *Newswrite*, Kids Book Review and *The School Magazine* and has been performed at Little Fictions.

TESS PEARSON writes poetry and prose, and has published microlit in Spineless Wonders' previous collections *Out of Place* (Spineless Wonders, 2015) and *Landmarks* (Spineless Wonders, 2017). She is currently working on a research project about literature and trauma.

MARK O'FLYNN's novel, *The Last Days of Ava Langdon*, was a finalist in the 2017 Miles Franklin Award. It has also been short listed for the Prime Ministers Literary Award for fiction, and is winner of the Voss Award 2017. His latest collection of poems is the chapbook *Shared Breath* (Hope Street Press, 2017).

CATHERINE NOSKE is a lecturer in Creative Writing and editor of *Westerly* Magazine at the University of Western Australia. Her current work, developed under a Varuna fellowship, was shortlisted for the 2015 Dorothy Hewett Award.

VENITA MUNIR is a Melbourne writer, editor and doctor. She has published microlit, short stories and music reviews, and her first novel manuscript was a finalist in the 2016 HARDCOPY program for fiction.

PAUL MUNDEN is Postdoctoral Research Fellow at the University of Canberra, and Director of the UK's National Association of Writers in Education (NAWE). He has published five collections of poetry, most recently *Chromatic* (UWAP, 2017).

MARJORIE LEWIS-JONES is an award-winning Sydney writer published by Spineless Wonders, ABC Radio National, Picaro Press, Poetry Australia, Cordite, Hunter Writers Centre, *Best Australian Writing 2015*, and other anthologies. She runs the literary blog, abiggerbrighterworld.com

DEBRA LE NEPVEU is a lawyer and an aspiring writer who is more fascinated by the personal stories driving court room conflict than the law. She is passionate about creating compelling, character-driven Australian fiction. She won the 2017 College of Law Essay Prize.

RAELEE LANCASTER is a Brisbane-based poet and research assistant. Raelee's poetry has appeared in *Rabbit* and *Westerly* and, in 2017, she was shortlisted for *Overland*'s Fair Australia Prize. Raised on Awabakal country, she has ties to the Wiradjuri people. @raeleelancaster.

JENNIFER KORNBERGER is a poet and writer of short fiction currently living in Fremantle, WA. Her work has been published in national journals and commended in the Newcastle Poetry Prize. She has just completed a second collection of poetry.

LEE KOFMAN is an award-winning author of four books, including the memoir *The Dangerous Bride*, and co-editor of *Rebellious Daughters*. Her next book, about imperfect bodies, will be out with Affirm Press. More at leekofman.com.au

SHARI KOCHER is the author of *The Non-Sequitur of Snow* (Puncher & Wattmann 2015), which was Highly Commended in the 2015 Anne Elder Awards. Recent awards include second place in the 2017 Newcastle Poetry Prize. carapacedreaming.wordpress.com

NIMITY JAMES studied writing at RMIT University. In 2016 she was awarded a Varuna's Writers Residential Fellowship. She lives in Melbourne.

ANDY JACKSON has featured at literary events and arts festivals in Australia, India, USA and Ireland. His most recent collection, *Music our bodies can't hold* (Hunter Publishers 2017), consists of portrait poems of other people with Marfan Syndrome.

EMMA HOMES grew up on a farm in Gippsland and later studied science at Melbourne University. She is an avid reader and book clubber. In 2016 she travelled through the Kimberley with her family.

RICHARD HOLT is a visual artist and a writer. His work has been included in National Flash Fiction Day anthologies and previous Spineless Wonders collections. He was cofounder of Melbourne zine store, Sticky. His debut collection, *What You Might Find* will be published in 2018 by Spineless Wonders. bigstorysmall.com.

TIM HEFFERNAN was awarded the 2016 joanne burns prize for his prose poem 'barunga conversations' and shortlisted in 2015 for 'butterflies in iraq'. He is co-editor of Verity La's, 'Clozapine Clinic - The Frater Project.'

DOMINIQUE HECQ grew up in the French-speaking part of Belgium, then moved to Melbourne to write a PhD on exile in Australian fiction. Some would say she's become one of the characters in the books she'd been reading. Dominique is the author of fifteen books, the latest being *Hush: A Fugue* (UWA Publishing, 2017).

MAREE GALLOP is a Newcastle award-winning writer and nurse. Her short stories appear in anthologies including; *Newcastle Short Story Award 2016* (Hunter Writers' Centre), *Landmarks* (Spineless Wonders, 2017), *Award Winning Australian Writing 2016 & 2017* (Melbourne Books).

LUKE FUSSELL is a writer and perpetual student currently living in Melbourne. He is proficient in one language.

YVONNE FEIN is a writer, playwright and editor and has been a lecturer at Australian Jewish Museum. Her novels include *April Fool*, *Torn Messiah* and *Rachel Racing Time*. She has won awards in Gotham Screenplay and Rhode Island Film Festivals.

LUKE EVANS was born and raised in Newcastle. After 20 years he left his hometown for Cairns, Qld. He has been a youth worker, a farmhand and a teacher. Nine years later he returned home.

JOHANNA ELLERSDORFER grew up in Sydney and works as a paintings conservator. Over the past ten years she has lived in various cities in Australia, Europe and the USA, and writes small stories in her spare time.

QUINN EADES is a researcher, writer, and award-winning poet, is the author of *all the beginnings: a queer autobiography of the body* (Australian Scholarly Publishing, 2015) and *Rallying (*UWA Publishing, 2017) and is currently working on a book written from the transitioning body, titled *Transpositions*.

CATHERINE DEERY lives in regional Victoria and is studying a Master of Creative Writing, Publishing and Editing. She usually writes longer stories, but is beginning to explore and play with microfiction.

SHADY COSGROVE is the author of *What the Ground Can't Hold* (Picador, 2013) and *She Played Elvis* (Allen and Unwin, 2009), which was shortlisted for the Australian Vogel Award. Her short fiction has appeared in *Best Australian Stories*, *Overland*, *Antipodes*, *Southerly* and other Spineless Wonders anthologies.

EILEEN CHONG is a Sydney poet. Her Australian books are *Burning Rice* (2012), *Peony* (2014), and *Painting Red Orchids* (2016), with Rainforest (2018) forthcoming. Her American book is *Another Language* (2017). eileenchong.com.au

JULIE CHEVALIER has written or co-edited six books of poetry and short fiction. *Darger: his girls* was awarded the Alec Bolton Prize for an Unpublished Poetry Manuscript, and shortlisted for the WA Premiers' Poetry Prize.

CHRISTINE BURROWS, a Melbourne poet, has appeared in many Australian and New Zealand anthologies and literary journals. Her work explores themes of grief, trauma, place, dislocation, social and environmental justice. Poetry keeps her going.

BRIANNA BULLEN is a Deakin University PhD candidate writing on memory in science fiction. She won the 2017 Apollo Bay short story competition and placed second in the 2017 Newcastle short story competition.

KATHLEEN BLEAKLEY has three collections with Ginninderra Press: *Azure*, 2017; *Lightseekers*, photography by 'pling, 2015; and *jumping out of cars*, with Andrea Gawthorne, images by 'pling, 2004.

AMANDA BERRY lives and teaches in Scone. Her writing has appeared in blogs, newspapers, videos and print. Her microfiction was shortlisted for the joanne burns Award in 2015 and 2016. Amanda loves long walks, jazz and Saturday afternoons.

EMMA ASHMERE's short stories have appeared in *The Age*, *Griffith Review, NGV Magazine*, Australian Review of Fiction, Landmarks (Spineless Wonders, 2107) and Brisbane billboards for #8WordStory. Her debut novel *The Floating Garden* (Spinifex Press, 2016) was a finalist in the Most Underrated Book Award.

DAEL ALLISON is a poet, fiction writer, essayist, editor and doctoral candidate in Creative Writing, University of Newcastle. She won the 2016 Spineless Wonders joanne burns Microlit Award, Hunter category. In 2017, she won The Philip Bacon Ekphrasis Award.

Editor

CASSANDRA ATHERTON is an award-winning writer, academic and critic. She is currently a Harvard Visiting Scholar in English. Her most recent books of prose poetry are *Trace* (Finlay Lloyd, 2015) and *Exhumed* (Grand Parade, 2015).

The joanne burns Award

Each year Spineless Wonders auspices an award for the best writing in the forms of prose poem and microfiction in honour of foremost Australian experimental poet, joanne burns. The award is open to people residing in Australia and to Australians living overseas. Finalists chosen by each year's judging panel are offered publication in our annual anthology alongside invited writers.

The inaugural *joanne burns Award* was held in 2011 and was judged by joanne burns who selected Charles D'Anastasi's 'Madame Bovary' as the winning entry and commended Erin Gough's 'William Shatner vows to save the Great Basin Pocket Mouse' and Clare McHugh's 'Briefly'. All three pieces, along with those of other finalists appear in *small wonder*, edited by Linda Godfrey and Julie Chevalier.

The *2012 joanne burns Award* was judged by Carol Jenkins who selected Mark O'Flynn's 'under the maw of luna park' as the winning entry and commended Richard Holt's 'bush burial', Trina Denner's 'playing outside', Stu Hatton's 'down south' and Paul Mitchell's 'The Old Man and the Pool'. The winner and finalists all appear in *Stoned Crows & other Australian Icons*, edited by Julie Chevalier and Linda Godfrey.

The *2013 joanne burns Award* was judged by Shady Cosgrove who selected Mark Smith's '10.42 to Sydenham' as the winning entry and Hilary Hewitt's 'happy' and Mark Robert's 'cities that are not Dublin' as runners-up. All three pieces, along with those of other finalists appear in *Writing to the Edge*, edited by Linda Godfrey and Ali Jane Smith.

In *2014, The joanne burns Award* was judged by Angela Meyer and Richard Holt who selected Susan McCreery's 'Hold Up' as the winning entry and Kirsten Tranter's 'Turing Test Study Guide' and Mark Smith's 'The Meteorologist's Daughter' as runners up. All three pieces, along with those of other finalists are published in *Flashing the Square*, edited by Linda Godfrey and Bronwyn Mehan.

The 2015 joanne burns Award was judged by Kirsten Tranter who selected Nick Couldwell's 'Dancing' as the winning entry. Runners up were Tim Heffernan for 'Butterflies in Iraq' and Matthew Gabriel for 'jesussaves82'. All three pieces, along with those of other finalists and invited contributors are published in *Out of Place* edited by Kirsten Tranter and Linda Godfrey.

The 2016 joanne burns Microlit Award was co-sponsored by the Newcastle Writers Festival. The national category, judged by Cassandra Atherton, was won by Tim Heffernan for 'Barunga Conversation' and the Newcastle category, judged by Karen Whitelaw and Joanna Atherfold Finn, was won by Dael Allison for 'Breakwall'. The winning entries and finalists from both categories as well as invited contributors are published in *Landmarks* edited by Cassandra Atherton.

The 2017 joanne burns Microlit Award was co-sponsored by the Newcastle Writers Festival and judged by Cassandra Atherton. The national category was won by Tess Pearson for 'Traces' and the Hunter category was won by Luke Evans for 'You Can't Go Back'. The winning entries and finalists from both categories as well as invited contributors are published in *Time* edited by Cassandra Atherton.

About joanne burns

joanne burns grew up in Sydney's eastern suburbs. She worked as an English teacher in New South Wales, and for a time in London. She has taught creative writing in tertiary institutions, schools and community organisations. Her first collection of poems, *Snatch*, was published in London in 1972. Since then she has published more than a dozen further books of poetry. Her poems have appeared in numerous Australian literary journals, poetry magazines and have been set for study on the Higher School Certificate syllabus. joanne has been particularly concerned with the blurring of the distinctions between poetry and prose in her work, and has written extensively in prose poem/ microfiction forms. She has also written monologues and short futurist fictions and 'farables' (fables/ parables).Her latest collection *Brush* was published by Giramondo Poets in 2014. In 2016, she was awarded the New South Wales Premiers' Kenneth Slessor Literary Award for Poetry.

More microlit from

SPINELESS WONDERS

A treasure trove of writing from some of the most innovative practitioners of prose poetry and microfiction in Australia.

KABITA DHARA, EDITOR, READINGS MONTHLY

Small Wonder

prose poems & microfiction

edited by Linda Godfrey and Julie Chevalier

Here are short and clever pieces by thirty contemporary Australian writers on the eroticism of mashed potato, parenting as magic realism and a tongue-in-cheek history of the Cyclops bicycle. Includes award-winning writers Michael Farrell, Keri Glastonbury, Judith Beveridge and Peter Boyle. Features prose poems and microfiction selected by competition judge joanne burns.

Illustrated by talented young artist, Paden Hunter.

'Sometimes serious, sometimes humorous, provocative, self-reflective and self-satirising, realist and stream of consciousness, this collection is above all a celebration of the many things Australia can mean to us.' JEAN BEDFORD, NEWTOWN REVIEW OF BOOKS

Stoned Crows

& other Australian Icons

prose poems & microfiction

edited by Linda Godfrey and Julie Chevalier

What do our best wordsmiths have to say about Australian icons? This anthology takes a fresh look at everything from the HIH collapse to crocs, Margaret Olley, bush burials and the ABC. We visit a post-apocalyptic Opera House and spend Saturday night in downtown Byron Bay. Tones range from nostalgic to sceptical, from wry to LOL. Featuring prose poems and microfiction by Mark O'Flynn, Anna Kerdijk Nicholson, Michael Sharkey, Moya Costello and many more.

'New voices, new ideas, refreshed old ones and all in degustation morsels from Melbourne to Marrakesh, from Sydney to Paris.'

KATHLEEN MARY FALLON

Writing to the Edge

prose poems & microfiction

edited by Linda Godfrey and Ali Jane Smith

If the art of the short story is knowing what to leave out, what is the art of microfiction? The 33 authors included in *Writing to the Edge* demonstrate many ways of making much from little. In pieces ranging in length from a few pages to a line or two, they intrigue, amuse, sadden and enlighten us in turn. Their carefully chosen words and striking images provide vivid glimpses into other lives, other places, other minds.

Emeritus Professor Elizabeth Webby AM

Flashing The Square

edited by Linda Godfrey & Bronwyn Mehan

This collection takes its name from an event at the Melbourne Writers Festival, where these miniature vignettes and mini-narratives were flashed on screens in Federation Square. There's a high standard of writing here across a broad range of subjects.The best contributions are full of potential and feeling: Susan McCreery's one-paragraph sketch of a service-station hold-up fills the reader with dread, and Michelle Wright's *Taken*, about a shark attack, with a kind of difficult grief. Ally Scale's *I Do* is heartbreaking and Shady Cosgrove's *Call an Ambulance* quite terrifying; for some reason the stories about unreasoning violence work best. Other contributors include such familiar names as Kirsten Tranter and A.S. Patric, as well as Angela Meyer.

Kerry Goldsworthy, SYDNEY MORNING HERALD

out
of
place
prose poems & microfiction
includes
Ceridwen Dovey
Rjurik Davidson
Tania Hershman
Roberta Lowing
Angela Meyer
John Tranter
edited by Kirsten Tranter & Linda Godfrey

Landmarks

edited by Cassandra Atherton

This anthology traverses areas from droughts, hunters, caring for elderly mothers and the burning of the Aboriginal flag to birthmarks, arms and even the desire to be Amelie.

Includes pieces from Indigenous writers, Sam Wagan Watson and Evelyn Araluen as well as writers concerned about the environment, reconciliation and life in contemporary Australia from remote and rural to innercity.

Spineless Wonders publications are available in print, digital and audio format from participating bookshops and online. For further information, go to the Spineless Wonders website:

www.shortaustralianstories.com.au

www.ingramcontent.com/pod-product-compliance
Lightning Source LLC
Chambersburg PA
CBHW050544190726
48284CB00003B/1195

* 9 7 8 1 9 2 5 0 5 2 3 5 0 *